FROM ME TO YOU

Paul Rogers

Pictures by Jane Johnson

ORCHARD BOOKS

For my mother

ORCHARD BOOKS
96 Leonard Street, London EC2A 4RH
Orchard Books Australia
14 Mars Road, Lane Cove, NSW 2066
ISBN 1 85213 035 0 (hardback)
ISBN 1 85213 860 2 (paperback)
First published in Great Britain 1987
First paperback publication 1995
Text © Paul Rogers 1987
Illustrations © Jane Johnson 1987
A CIP catalogue record for this book is available from the British Library.
Printed in Belgium

I came headfirst into this world
eighty years ago.
Inside, all lamps and firelight,
outside was white with snow.

Or so my mother told me.
What does a baby know?

Two brothers and a sister:
Harry, James and Tess.
And who's that in the christening robe —
that baby — can you guess?
My gran sewed all the lace by hand
on that little dress.

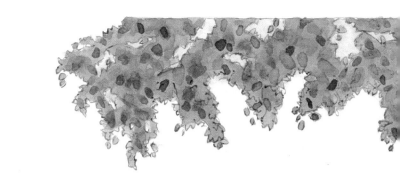

We had some fun, the four of us.
Once, we tossed a pie
in Mrs Morgan's knickers
hanging up to dry.

And Father spanked us one by one.
And I saw Harry cry.

James became a carpenter.   Harry went to sea.

And Tess became a lady and had us all to tea.

Alone at night, I used to dream
what might become of me.

I fell in love with Grandad.

My mother found that lace.

She pinned it round my wedding dress, then stitched it into place.

When Grandad turned to me in church,
you should have seen his face!

Soon we had a little girl,
born one summer's day.
I trimmed the tiny crib with lace,
where your mummy lay.

She was asleep beneath the tree when Grandad went away.

And now I'm getting very old.
Some things I just can't do —
like climb this hill! But I can still
stitch a thing or two.

Look what I've made with what was left.

Do you like it? It's for you.

FROM ME TO YOU is the story of a grandmother who was born in 1906. Her family was an ordinary, middle-class family, not poor and not rich. The small town they lived in was lit with gas light because they did not yet have electricity. The rooms of their house were heated with coal fires, as there was no central heating in the house and no plumbing except for cold running water in the kitchen. Water for baths was heated on the coal stove in the kitchen. People washed in wash basins and in tubs they filled by hand. Most clothes, especially clothes for children, were made at home. Boys wore big hats and short trousers until they were about twelve. Little girls always wore dresses, never dungarees, even when they went outdoors to play.

As is true in many large families, Gran's brothers and sisters grew up to have lives quite different from their parents and from each other. Her brother James worked as a carpenter. Harry went to sea as a ship's officer on an ocean-going liner, a large boat that carried passengers to and fro across the Atlantic. Tess married a rich man, but she didn't become too proud to love her brothers and sisters.

Gran was the youngest. She dreamed about what her future might hold because, while some women worked in the 1920's when she was a girl, they were considered to be suitable for only a few jobs and professions. Gran married Grandad, and, like many women before her, she settled down to keep house.

At last, in the late 1930's, Gran and Grandad's daughter was born. She was only three when Grandad went into the army in 1941 to fight in the Second World War. He never came home from that war. But his daughter — Gran's daughter — grew up, got married, and had a little girl of her own. Now Gran is sharing her memories of her life with her granddaughter. What is the story of *your* grandmother?